T0130562

# EMMITT'S AMAZING DAY

WRITTEN BY: NICOLE SMITH
ILLUSTRATED BY: JENNIFER SIEGAL

To order additional copies of this book, contact:
Xlibris
844-714-8691
www.Xlibris.com
Orders@Xlibris.com

ISBN:	Softcover	978-1-6641-8317-9
	Hardcover	978-1-6641-8316-2
	EBook	978-1-6641-8315-5

Library of Congress Control Number: 2021913301

Print information available on the last page

Rev. date: 08/04/2021

To my son Emmitt, who has taught me to love unconditionally and limitless patience, I love you deeply. Please always be yourself, exactly as you are, and remember that you are perfect.

Emmitt wakes up and stretches.
He makes his bed and gets dressed.
Rumble. Rumble.

He washes his face and
brushes his teeth.

Rumble. Rumble.

What's that noise?

Rumble

Rumble

It's coming from Emmitt's belly.
What shall he eat?

A doughnut?

Or a bowl of oatmeal with fresh blueberries?

He reaches for the oatmeal.

The oatmeal is warm in his
belly, and the blueberries
are sweet and delicious.
GOOD JOB, EMMITT!

Emmitt runs to catch the
school bus, and off he goes.

He feels great after his
healthy breakfast.
He sits at his desk. He is
calm and focused.
His teacher asks him a question.
It's hard, but he knows the answer.
He stands up and writes the answer
on the board. The whole class cheers!

AWESOME WORK, EMMITT!

It's time for music!
The music room is full
of instruments.
There are tambourines, guitars,
piano, and Emmitt's favorite–DRUMS!


Bang, bang, bang, ding.
Rumble. Rumble.

Bang, bang, bang, ding.
Rumble. Rumble.

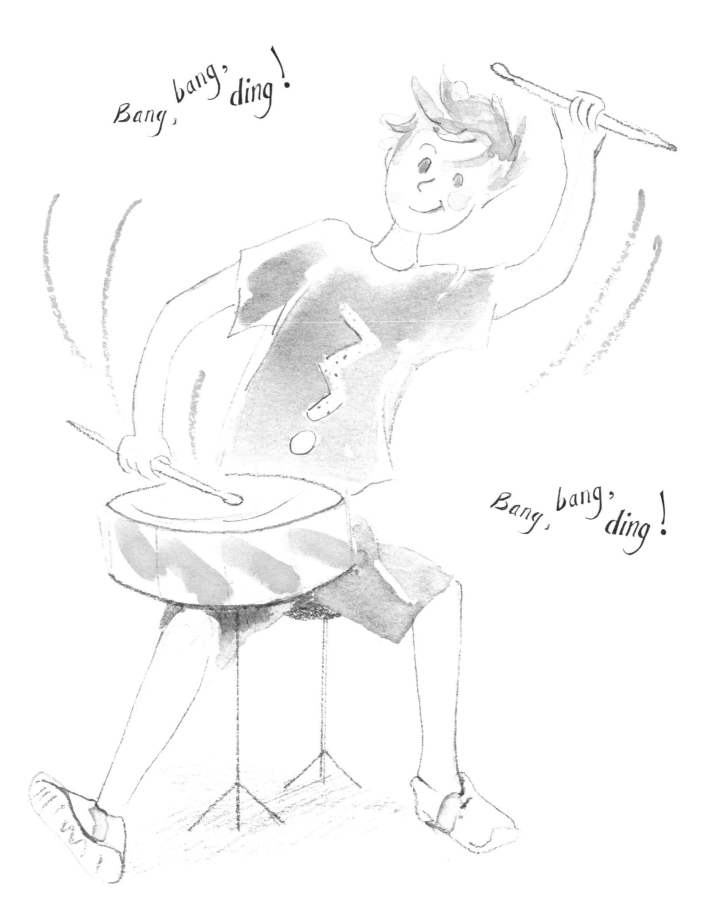

There's that noise again.

EMMITT is hungry.
What shall he eat?

The lunchroom has lots of choices.
The french fries smell yummy
but Emmitt remembers the last
time he ate fries. His tummy felt
yucky, and he was tired after.

He grabs a sandwich instead.

The sandwich is cool, crisp, and
a little salty. It is terrific!

WELL DONE, EMMITT!

Finally, it is time for the big soccer game. He has been excited about the game all day. Emmitt runs onto the soccer field. He has tons of energy from his healthy lunch.

He winds up and kicks the ball.
He is so strong. It soars through
the sky like a rocket ship.

GREAT JOB, EMMITT!
After the game, Emmitt goes home. He hears his tummy grumble again, and this time, he knows just what to do.

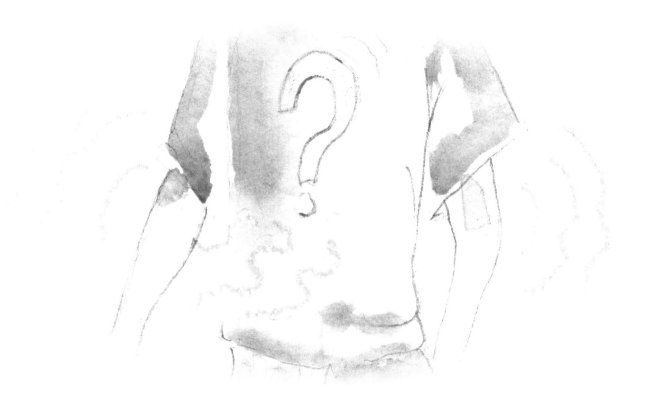

He looks around the kitchen and
sees a chocolate chip cookie and
a bright-red apple on the table.

The cookie is warm, and it smells
terrific, but he remembers
what a great day he had.

Why is today different
than other days?

Emmitt ate healthy foods all day!

He ate foods that were good for his body and good for his brain.

Emmitt reaches past the cookie and grabs the bright-red apple.

He takes a big, loud, juicy bite.

Chomp! Snap! Crunch! YUM!

He feels proud.

Emmitt's mom walks in and gives him a great, big hug. She tells him to put the apple down and hands him a cookie.

Emmitt is confused, and he asks his mom, "Why?"

She explains, "Emmitt, you were a superstar today! You were a good listener at school. You played well with your friends. You ate all your fruits and veggies. This cookie is a special treat. You earned it."

WAY TO GO, EMMITT!

Nicole Smith, the author of *Let's Start Brushing* and *Emmitt's Amazing Day*, grew up in a small beach town in Massachusetts. She is a loving wife and the mother of a picky eater. Her experience as a mom has driven her to write this book about healthy eating choices.

When she is not busy writing, she enjoys yoga, golf, and gardening. Please check out her work at facebook.com/BooksByNicoleSmith101 or on Instagram @booksbynicolesmith101

Jennifer Siegal is both an illustrator and traditional artist. She gains inspiration from nature and works in a variety of mediums, from pastel to oil to watercolor. Her work is on Instagram: @Jenny_Siegal_Art. She also is a member of the Palos Verdes Art Center's the Artist Studio Gallery. Visit www.TASPV.com to see more of her work or send commission inquiries to RedondoJenny@gmail.com.

Printed in the United States
by Baker & Taylor Publisher Services